IMAGINE THAT

Licensed exclusively to Imagine That Publishing Ltd
Tide Mill Way, Woodbridge, Suffolk, IP12 1AP, UK
www.imaginethat.com
Copyright © 2023 Imagine That Group Ltd
All rights reserved
0 2 4 6 8 9 7 5 3 1
Manufactured in China

Written by Ellie Wharton
Illustrated by Maxine Lee

ISBN 978-1-80105-658-8

A catalogue record for this book is available from the British Library

Hungry Monster!

Ellie Wharton

Maxine Lee

Milly ran down the stairs two at a time. She had seen something rather alarming from her bedroom window and she had to tell Mum as fast as she could.

'**Quick, Mum!**' she shouted. 'Hide all the china, hang the pots and pans out of reach ... Hungry Monster is coming to dinner!'

But Mum was as cool as a cucumber and carried on cooking.

Hungry Monster knocked on the door.

Milly opened the door just a crack, but Hungry Monster pushed it open and bumbled in.

He tipped the hats off the hat stand, knocked over a vase of flowers and **crashed** into the kitchen.

Milly followed him open-mouthed.

'Do sit down,' said Milly's mum, calmly.

But Hungry Monster didn't just sit down.
He threw himself down with a thump and broke the chair.

Milly's *mum* offered him a bigger one.

'**Huummmphhh!**' frowned Hungry Monster.

Then, '**Garummmmpppphh!**' he groaned, banging his fists down on the table.

Milly couldn't believe Hungry Monster's bad manners. But Mum just put a plate of food down gently in front of him ...

... and then another ...

and another ...

and another.

Clever Mum had made all of
Hungry Monster's favourite food!

He guzzled down beans on toast ...

followed by
pizza and then

a meat and
potato dinner ...

... then jelly and ice cream for dessert,

all washed down with a WHOLE jug of fizzy lemonade!

'BURRRRRRRRRRRRRRRRPPPPPPP!'

went Hungry Monster.

Mum laughed. Milly laughed.
Hungry Monster's frown
began to turn upside down ...

He wasn't hungry any more!

And when Hungry Monster wasn't hungry he was happy!

He danced the tango with Mum ...

But soon Hungry Monster was hungry again and his smile began to fade ...

Rumble, groan grumble ...

Luckily, clever Mum was always one step ahead.

'Quick!' she said.
'Show him the door, Milly!
I've told him it's time for milk and cookies next door at Tabitha's!'